WOMEN'S RIGHTS AT WORK

WOMEN IN THE WORLD™

WOMEN'S RIGHTS AT WORK

ZOE LOWERY AND JERI FREEDMAN

Rosen YA™
New York

Published in 2018 by The Rosen Publishing Group, Inc.
29 East 21st Street, New York, NY 10010

First Edition

Library of Congress Cataloging-in-Publication Data

Names: Lowery, Zoe, author. | Freedman, Jeri, author.
Title: Women's rights at work / Zoe Lowery and Jeri Freedman.
Description: First Edition. | New York : Rosen Publishing, [2018] | Series: Women in the world | Audience: Grade 7 to 12. | Includes bibliographical references and index.
Identifiers: LCCN 2017010120 | ISBN 9781508174516 (library bound : alk. paper)
Subjects: LCSH: Discrimination in employment—Juvenile literature. | Sex discrimination against women—Juvenile literature. | Women—Employment—Juvenile literature. | Wages—Women—Juvenile literature.
Classification: LCC HD4903 .L69 2018 | DDC 331.4—dc23
LC record available at https://lccn.loc.gov/2017010120

Manufactured in the United States of America

CONTENTS

NTRODUCTION

The US Department of Labor, reports that women made up about 47 percent of the workforce in 2012. Accounting for nearly half of the working population might suggest that women are also about equal within the workplace. Alas, they do not. Many women still take home a smaller paycheck than men and are presented with fewer opportunities at work.

Unfortunately, male managers maintain misgivings about hiring and promoting women, particularly when it comes to high-level positions. Lower starting salaries and less pay for the same work men do in the same position is the norm.

Taking full advantage of women and using them as a source of cheap labor is by no means an issue exclusive to Canada and the United States. In fact, in every country on the planet, women workers make less money than their male counterparts. Industries all over the world need people to do jobs that require little skill. Garment manufacturing continues to work as a means for women to begin working out of the home in countries such as Asia, Latin America and Sub-Saharan Africa. Here, according to the International Labor Rights Forum, women make up anywhere from 70 percent to 90 percent of the labor force. Women are also instrumental in producing many common household items used today, electronics, and agricultural supplies.

Meanwhile, while working outside the home offers new choices and financial freedom, the rights of these working women are often neglected as they deal with on-the-job harassment, both physical and sexual, are coerced into taking pregnancy tests, and denied promotions and other benefits simply because of their gender. They also suffer with wage theft and are unable to unionize. Meanwhile, many women are still expected to defer to men within their homes, which forces them to work even more once they get home. Other women struggle to raise their children on their own and may not be able to give their children the amount of guidance they need. Violence against women has increased as well. They are far more often fired for simply getting married or pregnant, are denied contracts that would guarantee their positions, and are forced to endure dangerous working conditions.

Tens of millions of domestic workers, for example, many of whom are migrants or even children, around the world are exploited with low pay and excessive working hours. Some are practically imprisoned—unable to leave the homes in which they work—and suffer abuse.

Women's rights in the workplace have been strengthened and supported over the last few decades thanks to the passage of legislation.

In addition to unequal treatment on the job, women are vulnerable to sexual harassment—ranging from unwelcome advances to off-color jokes and snide remarks from men who resent or are threatened by their presence.

In spite of near-constant hurdles, working women have made some progress in the last several decades. Laws have been passed to help women in the workplace. Some companies are taking steps to protect and support women's equality, including provisions for their LGBTQ+ employees.

CHAPTER 1

JOINING THE WORKFORCE

Over hundreds of years, cultural and religious mindsets have formed the ways in which we look at women and their work. Although those attitudes seem antiquated to us today, they continue to affect today's perception of modern women in the workforce.

PREINDUSTRIAL WORK

In the early days of America and Canada, men and women generally worked together in family businesses. On the frontier, farming was the predominant enterprise, both in the colonies and later in the early 1800s during the expansion into the western part of North America. This meant that strength and hardiness were the most desirable traits for both women and men. Women cared for home and children, and men were more likely to be involved in jobs requiring physical strength, such as building barns. But people of both genders cleared land, planted crops, and tended livestock.

Off the farm, men were likely to be active in trades that earned significant money, such as shipbuilding, brewing, printing, and merchant shipping. Women were primarily involved in caring for home and children. There were a limited number of trades that were primarily engaged in by women. Women were milliners, who made hats, and seamstresses, who

Fig. 71. — Atelier de modistes, d'après une gravure de Bosio.

In the 1800s, opportunities for women to work out of the house were scant, but they could be employed in trades such as milliners, making hats.

made clothing items for sale, such as aprons and shirts. Women also made items for sale, such as candles and soap. Businesses like these were seen as acceptable for women because they were a natural outgrowth of "women's work." However, men ran the major businesses. Because men made most of the money, they retained most of the power, and ran the business of the colonies and the countries that grew out of them.

INDUSTRIAL AGE WORK

Prior to the mid-nineteenth century, most work that women performed was done inside the home, performed in someone else's home, or was an extension of traditional women's work done outside the home. In-home work consisted of doing laundry or sewing, providing childcare, or taking in boarders. Through the first quarter of the twentieth century, it was common for both middle-class and upper-class households to employ servants. Many women served as maids, cooks, and other household help, either on a live-in or daily basis, often beginning employment as young girls. Even nurses in hospitals were basically servants whose job it was to clean up and tend patients' basic needs.

The Industrial Revolution changed the way that many women—and men—worked. The term "Industrial Revolution" refers to the rise of technology beginning near the end of the eighteenth century that led to the shift from making things by hand to making them by machines in factories. The Industrial

Most nineteenth-century working women were employed in areas that aligned with their traditional roles, such as servants. They also worked in sewing and textiles.

Revolution changed the way people lived and worked. Prior to the Industrial Revolution, most goods were made by individual craftspeople and sold or bartered for goods locally. Now, for the first time, people who owned factories and employed large numbers of people as workers controlled the production of goods. The chance to work in the city attracted workers from farms and small towns. Factories also provided a means of livelihood to the flood of immigrants who came to the United States and Canada during the nineteenth and early twentieth centuries. Women were not limited only to "women's work." Even in the nineteenth century, women were documented as working in five hundred different trades, including driving carts and being bridge keepers. However, most women who were employed outside the home generally worked in traditional female areas, such as laundries or textile factories. In the mid-1800s, the most predominant occupation for women was servant, followed by the sewing and textile trades. Many worked in textile mills, where cloth was made, and in clothing factories. Prior to World War II, women were generally prohibited from learning many skills necessary for obtaining better-paying jobs that were occupied by men—and from applying for such jobs. This allowed factory owners to guarantee a pool of workers who had no choice but to work for low pay, which benefited the owners by reducing costs and increasing profits.

SWEATING AND SEWING

In the nineteenth and early twentieth centuries, work in factories was harsh. Women, often young girls, frequently worked extremely long hours. The factories were often poorly heated in the winter and sweltering in the summer. In the days before labor and workplace safety laws, factories were often dangerous places to work. Such factories, where employees were forced to work long hours in terrible conditions over which they had no control, were called sweatshops.

(continued on the next page)

Factory work in the 1800s and early 1900s could be harsh, including extreme temperatures, long hours, and no insurance if workers were injured.

(continued from the previous page)

There were no protections or insurance for workers, and if one became injured, she was simply dismissed to fend for herself.

The largest area of employment for women in the nineteenth and early twentieth centuries, aside from being a servant, was working in the sewing trades. In textile mills, where cloth was made, 60 percent of the workers were girls and women. And in many clothing factories, all or most of the workers were female—although supervisors were male. As far as the factory owners were concerned, women were the ideal employees for tasks that required dexterity (skill with one's hands) and attention to detail, rather than brute strength. In addition, women were willing to work for lower wages than men, which was appealing to mill and factory owners. And women were raised to be docile, so they were unlikely to make trouble over their working conditions.

A second group of women who worked outside the home were those in the retail trade (selling goods to people). In the preindustrial period, when most shops were family-owned, women worked alongside their husbands in businesses like inns and shops selling pottery, clothing, food, and other such goods. As the industrial age brought increasing prosperity to a growing middle class, the demand for goods increased. Many family businesses such as Macy's grew into major commercial enterprises, and new stores were opened to meet the rising demand. Women were rarely seen in managerial positions in these businesses. Instead, they were hired as "shopgirls," whose job it was to stand behind counters in department stores, be charming, and sell items to customers. Again, as their job was waiting on customers, they were still placed in servant-like roles.

STEREOTYPES

The view that men's role was to work outside the home and earn money, and women's role was to take care of home and children and provide support for their men, influenced how women were perceived in the workplace. The predominant attitude in the industrial age was that women's work was temporary. They would leave to get married or raise children, which was viewed by most people as women's proper work. For example, both young men and young women might be hired to work as salespeople in department stores, but when a chance for promotion came up, the young man would be chosen because the boss assumed that the girl would eventually leave to get married. Indeed, it was considered socially unacceptable for a wealthy or middle-class woman to work because this implied that her husband was unable to support her, which made him look bad. If a woman wished to do something outside the home, she was expected to engage in charity work.

As is typical with most stereotypes, the reality behind women's reasons for working conflicted with what people thought. Middle-class and upper-class women were free to lavish their time on home and family as they wished, whereas millions of working-class women were forced to balance raising children and working, whether in factories or by taking in work at home. Men reaped the benefits of perpetuating the idea that women need not work: all the better to keep the jobs that paid more for themselves. Furthermore, women's dependence on men ensured that men always had someone at home who was ready to look after their every desire, which meant that they were at liberty to go outside the home to pursue their aspirations however they liked.

MODERN WORKING WOMEN

CHAPTER 2

The realities of the Second World War drew women into the workforce like never before. What followed was both liberating and confining, and the new challenge of fighting for women's rights in the workplace was brought front and center.

SECOND WORLD WAR ROOTS

The modern role of women in the workforce has its roots in World War II (1939–1945). During World War II, women entered the mainstream workforce in large numbers for the first

Rosie the Riveter symbolized women who joined the workforce to help keep the economy humming while so many men were fighting in the Second World War.

time. Because so many men were in the military, there was a shortage of workers in many jobs. In addition, when the United States entered the war, it needed vast amounts of supplies and equipment. At the same time that factories were gearing up to increase production, they were losing a large percentage of their mainly male workforce. Women were encouraged to step up to fill those jobs. “Rosie the Riveter” became the new symbol of the American woman pitching in to keep the wartime economy going, doing her patriotic duty to support the war effort by working in jobs that ranged from office work to assembling parts for aircraft and other military equipment. Rosie was actually Rose Will Monroe, a riveter at the Willow Run Aircraft factory in Ypsilanti, Michigan. She was featured in a promotional film and poster campaign. The number of women in the workforce increased 57 percent from 1940 to 1944.

Many of the women who took jobs were young, and working helped shaped their attitudes about themselves. Entering the workforce had two effects on American women: It gave them a sense of self-confidence that they could indeed do many jobs as well as men, despite having been told for generations that they couldn’t, and it gave them financial independence—they could buy their own necessities and treat themselves to things that they wanted. Despite attempts in the 1950s to turn back the clock, as discussed in the next section, attitudes were being changed forever. Equal work didn’t mean equal pay, however. In 1942, the National War Board pressured companies to voluntarily increase the pay for women to the rate paid to men when they were doing the same jobs with the same quality. Most companies were more interested in their profits than in women's rights, so they refused to voluntarily increase the pay rate for female workers. Women's pay remained unequal.

POSTWAR EFFECTS

The influx of women into the workplace didn't last, however. The end of the war brought waves of men returning from the military to civilian life—and they wanted jobs. In many cases, women were dismissed from their jobs to make way for the returning men. Because there were no legal protections, many companies gave preference to men over women applying for the same jobs. The government asked women to voluntarily give up their jobs to returning soldiers. As wartime production shut down, the number of jobs shrank. The government feared that, if women kept jobs, there wouldn't be enough for men, and this high unemployment would lead to a depression (a period in which business declines because people can't afford to buy goods). In addition, many women left the workforce to have children now that the war was over and their husbands had returned, creating the "baby boom" generation. Television shows such as *Father Knows Best, Leave It to Beaver*, and others promoted

Television programs like *Leave it to Beaver* showed the "ideal" family, in which the mother always cared for her family.

the image of the perfect family with a stay-at-home mother taking care of her husband and children.

Nonetheless, women's attitudes toward working were changing, and a quarter of married women continued to work outside the home. By 1956, 35 percent of the workforce was women. However, working did not mean equality. Those girls and women who did work in the 1950s were paid on average 59 to 64 cents for every dollar a man earned. Companies claimed that men had to support families, while women only needed money for luxuries.

REPRESENTING WOMEN AND MINORITIES

The 1950s were a prosperous time for many Americans—especially if they were white, male, and middle-class. Members of minority groups, especially African Americans, didn't share in this prosperity. Segregation (keeping black people separate from white people) was legal. African Americans were not allowed into many facilities that were used by whites, and those that were provided for them were often inferior. In addition, they were denied many opportunities that were available only to white people. In response to this injustice, the civil rights movement formed with the goal of gaining equal treatment under the law for

African Americans. After many violent confrontations and legal actions, a number of laws were enacted, eliminating segregation and outlawing discrimination on the basis of gender as well as color. Passing a law and changing social attitudes so that people comply with the spirit of the law are two different matters, however. Although antidiscrimination laws enacted in the 1960s forbade discrimination in hiring, many managers and companies continued to hire primarily white men for managerial and professional positions. Women and minorities had a hard time getting hired for, or being promoted to, high-paying positions. Proving discrimination was difficult. Choosing a candidate to hire or promote is often a matter of personal judgment, which makes it difficult to prove in court that a candidate was not chosen because of gender or color. Nonetheless, it was easy to document that women, blacks, and members of other minority groups were underrepresented at higher levels of responsibility. Therefore, the federal government instituted affirmative action.

Affirmative action refers to the set of formal programs legislated by the federal government that are designed to increase the number of women and minorities hired to the same level as whites and men. A similar initiative enacted in Canada is called employment equity. Affirmative action regulations do

The goal of affirmative action is to ensure that minorities are hired at the same rate as white and male workers, but opponents question if it is entirely fair.

not require companies to hire women at all costs. They merely require that when two candidates are equally qualified, the woman or minority candidate be given preference until a reasonable percentage of employees are women or minorities. Those in favor of affirmative action believe it is crucial to ensuring that women and minorities are given equal opportunity because many people are still prejudiced against them. Opponents of affirmative action claim that it is sometimes unfair to white male candidates, and that while it served a purpose at one time, times have changed and it is no longer necessary.

POSITIVE CHANGES

According to the *Affirmative Action Review* of 1995 by Senior Adviser to the President for Policy and Strategy George Stephanopoulos and Special Counsel to the President Christopher Edley Jr., from the early 1900s to the mid-1970s, women earned on average about 60 percent of what men earned. Much of this difference in earnings is attributable to the fact that women were in lower-paying jobs.

Throughout most of the twentieth century, girls and women were restricted to low-paying jobs. Prior to the 1970s, women in some states were forbidden by law from employment in certain fields, such as firefighting, police work, and mining. In some cities, women were prohibited from even applying for jobs as police officers or firefighters, and this was completely legal. Want ads often specified that applicants had to be male.

There were no laws to protect girls and women from sexual harassment or from being fired simply because they got married or became pregnant. On one hand, male managers often assumed that women would leave if they got married or pregnant in order to take care of their children. On the other hand, women were often fired for a variety of reasons if they became pregnant or got married. For instance, many men felt that women should have children and devote themselves to taking care of them if they were married. They also believed that women wouldn't dedicate themselves to their jobs as fully if they also had a family. In certain professions, such as teaching, it was considered inappropriate to have pregnant women in front of children because it raised issues relating to sex. Finally, many men considered it OK for a woman to work if she was single because she had to support herself. But if she got married, she'd have a husband to support her, and continuing to work meant that she was taking a job from a man who might have a family to support.

Although laws prohibiting employment discrimination were passed in the 1960s, it wasn't until the late 1970s that women really started to make progress in the workplace, achieving better jobs and higher pay. One reason for this was that changing the law is often not sufficient to achieve a major cultural change in attitudes. For example, if a girl applied for an after-school job at a hardware store or garage, she would only be hired for a position as a cashier because it was assumed that she didn't know anything about using tools. It is also necessary to change the way that society views a group of people such as women—and often more important—the way that people view themselves. This is the role played by the women's movement.

THE FEMINIST MOVEMENT

The women's movement, or the feminist movement, refers to the organized efforts of women from the nineteenth century to the present to change social attitudes about women and obtain equal treatment for them in areas such as work. The fight to secure the right to vote is known as the "first wave" of feminism, and the women's movement in the 1960s and 1970s is known as the "second wave." The debate over fairness in the workplace is not new. As far back as 1923, women's rights advocates hotly debated women's wages. That year in *Adkins v. Children's Hospital*, the US Supreme Court struck down a Washington, D.C., law that set a minimum wage for women workers. The court ruled that the law was unconstitutional because if one allowed the state to set a minimum wage, it could also theoretically set a maximum wage, and setting a specific wage interfered with the right of people to freely negotiate their pay. Women's rights advocates were arrayed on both sides of the argument, some arguing that the D.C. law at least guaranteed the women workers a minimum wage

Betty Friedan was a force to be reckoned with in the feminist movement. In addition to writing, she helped found NOW (National Organization for Women).

and others fearing it would lead to a set, lower rate of pay for women.

Today, working women have more laws to support their protection against sexual harassment and abuse, as well as more equal opportunity and wages, thanks to the increasingly strong woman's movement. Betty Friedan's *The Feminine Mystique* (1963) and other feminist texts played a part in the post-war cultural swing that prompted more women to look for jobs as well as feminist movement's the second surge.

CHAPTER 3

WOMEN'S EQUALITY

When you have the same chance to be hired and eventually promoted at your job, you have an equal opportunity. This term means the same kind of workplace treatment, whether you are male or female. It remains an elusive goal so far, but one well worth the struggle.

HIRING HURDLES FOR GIRLS AND WOMEN

The first hurdle that girls and women face in the workplace is getting hired. The key law that protects women's rights in the workplace is Title VII of the Civil Rights Act of 1964 (usually just referred to as Title VII). This act covers employees of businesses with fifteen or more employees and state and local government agencies.

Studies show that women and girls work much harder to get the jobs they want, sending out more résumés, applying for more jobs, and going to more interviews than men.

It doesn't cover federal government employees or outside contractors. Title VII prohibits discrimination based on race, skin color, gender, religious beliefs, or national origins. Such discrimination applies to hiring, promotions, work assignments, benefits, and virtually every other aspect of employment. In 2014, then–President Barack Obama signed an executive order that prevents any business working with the federal government from discriminating against anyone because of their sexual orientation and gender identity. Federal employees are also protected against discrimination based on their gender identity thanks to this order.

Unfortunately, girls and women often have to send out more resumes, respond to more ads, and attend more interviews to obtain a job. In many cases, women are also offered less for a given job than a male candidate, possibly because of the belief on the part of the manager doing the hiring that women will accept less money than a male candidate. Some of the reasons for this are discussed later in this resource.

DISCRIMINATING QUESTIONS (AND HOW TO ANSWER THEM)

When it comes to hiring, it is illegal for potential employers to ask certain questions that could lead to discriminating against a woman because of characteristics related to her gender or gender identity. Among these questions are those related to the following:

- Age: Could be used to see if a woman is of childbearing age, among other things; employers may ask if a person is a minimum age for jobs that require it, such as serving alcohol.

(continued on the next page)

(continued from the previous page)

- **Pregnancy:** Such as, "Do you plan to have children?"
- **Family:** Such as, "Do you have children?" and "Do you have people at home you take care of?" They can ask if a person is available for certain shifts or timeframes.
- **Marital status:** Such as, "Are you married?" and "Do you plan to get married?"
- **Height or weight:** They can ask if a person is able to carry out specific required physical tasks.

What is the best way for a person to respond if she is asked an illegal question? Responding in a defensive way is likely to keep her from getting the job. The best way is to answer the question behind the question. In other words, if someone asks a person if she has children at home that she has to take care of, the best answer is probably something like, "I understand that the job may require me to work hours other than strictly nine to five, and I'm prepared for that." If the question, although illegal, was asked out of legitimate concern that the individual might be running out the door the minute the clock strikes five, when that person may still be needed, that answer should address the issue. If the interviewer keeps asking inappropriate questions, however, that may indicate a prejudicial attitude toward hiring a woman.

ADVERSITIES TOWARD ADVANCEMENT

Once a woman has a job, she has to deal with the issue of advancement. All too often, however, girls and women run into discrimination when it comes to promotions. A number of recent studies shed light on the differences between the opportunities for men and women in corporations.

According to an article by J. D. McCullough for The Guardian, some of the foremost international companies in the United States, Asia, and Europe seem to have done little more than symbolically place women in top executive positions. A study by the UK's global gender consulting firm 20-first revealed that two women sit in top executive committees in 60 percent of US corporations, and eight were CEOs in corporations including IBM, Pepsi Corporation, and General Motors. Nevertheless, men are still overwhelmingly at the helm of most companies at 83 percent. In Europe that number jumps to 89 percent and spikes in Asia to 89 percent. All told, the numbers add up to an unimpressive 11 percent of executive committee positions held by women in these three major regions.

One issue that affects the promotion of women in corporations is their attitude. In general, women are more likely than men to be brought up to think

Middle management women tend to worry more than men do about striking a healthy balance between work and home, and hold more of the childrearing responsibilities.

about others, whereas boys are raised to think about achievement. Boys are constantly pushed into competing and winning. This plays out in the corporate world as well.

Interestingly, women in middle management are more likely than men to worry about balancing home life and work. But at the senior management level, men are more likely than women to be worried by this. Age may be a key element in this fact. Women are typically in middle management when they are in their thirties and, therefore, likely to have young children. Like it or not, women still bear the brunt of childrearing responsibilities, even when they work. And this is the about the same time that managers single out potential individuals for the top spots. By the time most people reach senior management, they are middle-aged. Many middle-aged women are free of responsibilities for raising children. At the same time, many middle-aged men, who have devoted their entire lives to their job, start to feel a need for other types of fulfillment, including spending more time with their family. However, it is also true that a larger proportion of women than men who make it to senior management are unmarried or divorced.

According to Catalyst (an organization that seeks to advance women's role in business) in 2016 women held 23 (4.6 percent) of CEO positions at S&P 500 companies. Moving down the ranks, women made up 9.5 percent of the highest earners, nearly 20 percent of board seats, about 25 percent of executives or senior officials and managers, around 36 percent of first or mid-level managers and officials, and about 44 percent of total employees in S&P 500 companies.

Advancement in leadership positions, are hindered in a number of ways, says Deborah Gillis of Catalyst: "They are less likely to be given access to the assignments they need to advance—"hot jobs" such as visible assignments and mission-critical roles. In addition, women are also unwittingly subject to the double-bind, whereby because they are often evaluated against a "masculine" standard of leadership, women are left with limited and unfavorable options, no matter how they behave and perform as leaders."

STRUGGLING AGAINST THE GLASS CEILING

The "glass ceiling" refers to an invisible barrier that stops a woman's upward progress. In business, this refers to a barrier that keeps a woman from being promoted beyond a certain level simply because she is female. The barrier is invisible because it is not an official policy but discrimination resulting from the personal prejudices and opinions of senior management. Often, this barrier becomes apparent when a woman has advanced to a certain level, usually middle management.

In a recent study published in the *Journal of Applied Psychology*, Karen S. Lyness and Madeline E. Heilman examined 448 women managers. They found that women were promoted to senior management less frequently than men. Beyond that, they found that women who were promoted to senior management had better performance reviews than men who were promoted, and their promotion was more closely tied to outstanding performance. What this implies is that a man may be promoted to the highest levels for many reasons. He may be perceived as having "what it takes" or "leadership qualities." For a woman to get promoted, her performance must be extraordinary.

The authors of the study suggested that one reason for the difficulty women have with breaking into senior management is the perception on the part of those running the company, or sitting on the board of directors, that women have certain stereotypical characteristics that would interfere with their ability to perform at the highest levels of management. Examples of such stereotypes are "women are emotional" and "women will put their families before their job." Women are seen as "caring" and "relationship-oriented," but men are seen as tough and aggressive—attitudes that men doing the promoting see as critical to succeeding. The authors showed that stereotypical assumptions about women colored the way that senior management evaluated women. They tended to interpret women's behavior in the workplace in light of what they assumed about women. In other words, if a man goes out of his way to show a subordinate how to do something, he's being a mentor; if a woman does so, she's being caring or "touchy-feely." Thus, similar behavior is interpreted differently according to gender. Or if a man objects strongly to something, he's seen as being "forceful" or "assertive," whereas a woman doing the same thing is seen as being unreasonable or "overemotional." Thus, biased attitudes work against women two ways. A woman faces the assumption that she doesn't have "what it takes" based on preconceptions by senior management. This view is then justified by her performance reviews, in which her behavior is interpreted according to these same preconceptions.

Breaking through the glass ceiling is extremely difficult, and women in this position are often faced with hard choices. Should they try to behave like the stereotype of a man—in an aggressive and tough fashion? Should they admit that they have no chance of getting promoted and go to another company or start their own business? Should they attempt to collect evidence of discrimination and try to implement a complaint through the Equal Employment Opportunity Commission (EEOC) or a lawsuit for discrimination? Unfortunately, the only real remedy for the glass ceiling is a change in attitudes throughout society so that people are valued equally for their skills, regardless of gender.

MIRED IN THE PINK-COLLAR GHETTO

The "Pink-Collar Ghetto" refers to the pool of low-paying, dead-end jobs in fields populated mostly by girls and women. This category includes jobs such as waitress, grocery store cashier, childcare worker, nurse's aide, clerical worker, house and office cleaner, and hotel housekeeping staff, among others.

One aspect that pink-collar jobs have in common is that they are seen as "women's work." Another is that the pay is frequently low and benefits often limited or nonexistent. One reason why pay is low is that this type of work frequently involves serving or caring for people, and such work is looked down upon in our society. Another is that women are often desperate to find work to pay their bills but possess few job skills. Therefore, they will take jobs at low pay that men will not. A third reason is that even unskilled men can often find higher-paying work in jobs that are dangerous or require physical strength, like construction or mining. Such industries may have difficulty finding people willing to do dangerous, physically demanding work and so must pay higher wages. Even when men and women do essentially the same job, women's jobs are frequently presented as less significant, reflecting their different status in American society. Thus, a man who cleans a building is a janitor, but a woman who does so is a cleaning lady or maid—and it's likely that the man is paid more.

Because the pay for women is so low in the pink-collar ghetto, many women must work two, or even three, jobs to make ends meet. Having to work so much, and often care for children as well, means they do not have the time to learn new skills that would lead to better jobs, even if they had the money to attend classes.

Because skilled and semiskilled jobs in trades that are primarily male pay significantly more than jobs in predominately female fields, the US government passed the Nontraditional Employment for Women (NEW) Act of 1991. This act requires state job-training agencies to put in place programs to train women for nontraditional jobs, for example, carpentry or truck driving. Nontraditional fields are defined as those where fewer than 25 percent of those employed are women.

TRUCKIN' DOWN THE MOMMY TRACK

The "mommy track" refers to an alternate career path for women in their prime who raise children as well as work. Many women must make a choice that men do not. Do they devote themselves fully to their career, or do they devote themselves primarily to the children and merely work to earn money? Many women choose to take time off to have children and care for them while they are growing up. Those who need to work as well as care for a family must often take time off from their jobs or work fewer hours, which reduces their chances of advancement in corporate life. Of course, some women successfully blance both motherhood and a career.

More companies offer more flexibility, such as working from home, a benefit of particular help to moms. These benefits don't necessarily lead to promotions to high levels, however.

Many companies have taken steps to "keep talented female employees" who have family responsibilities. These include elements such as providing for childcare, offering flexible hours, and allowing employees to work remotely over a computer from home. While these steps are beneficial in that they help women retain professional positions in the workplace, nonetheless, the mommy track is a road that often (but not always) forks away from the executive suite. Women on the mommy track may have a more difficult time getting promoted to high levels of authority because these jobs are considered to require a greater level of availability to the business and a willingness to work whatever hours are necessary to achieve a goal. More and more women are becoming successful businesswomen while raising their families, however, in spite of these challenges.

Through the years, the wage gap, or statistical measure of the difference between the average pay for women and men, has gotten progressively smaller. Although that's terrific news, more recently, the DOL reports that progressed has slowed. Women still have a ways to go before achieving workplace equality.

MYTHS AND FACTS

MYTH: Because the number of women in middle management has been steadily increasing, women and men will eventually reach equality in the workplace.

FACT: According to the Department of Labor, in 2016 fewer than one in three women made up executive positions and other high-paying positions. For example, slightly more than one in six women are working as software developers in 2016.

MYTH: If you work hard and do a good job, you will be promoted.

FACT: Doing good work is not enough. Management's attitudes and corporate "politics" often play a major role in who gets promoted to key positions. Women need to learn how to present themselves and their accomplishments to gain the attention of key management.

MYTH: Today, working men and women share household and childcare tasks equally.

FACT: A 2014 US Department of Labor survey found that working women spend more than 2 hours per day doing household activities compared to less than 1.5 hours spent by men.

CHAPTER 4

EQUALITY AND PROTECTION IN PAY AND WORK

Over the years, a number of court cases and laws have stepped up women's protection and equality in the workplace. In many ways, great strides have been made, but in others women still have a long way to go.

Within the LGBTQ community, for example, workplace discrimination is still rampant. The United States does not have a federal law offering them protection. According to Catalyst.org, only twenty-nine of the fifty states offer any protections based on sexual orientation. Only thirty-three states offer gender identity protection. So in many states employees can be fired just for being transgender or

LGB. A number of top companies do offer benefits to employees who are LGBTQ+.

Employment discrimination based on sexual orientation is outlawed in sixty-one countries. In some countries, however, such as India, a same-sex relationship is illegal. In these cases they cannot be protected at work, either. About one-fifth of lesbian, gay, or bisexual people in France and Germany had to deal with discrimination either on the job or during their search for a new job. Meanwhile 90 percent of transgender people were provoked or abused at work because of their gender identity.

THE GAPING WAGE GAP

Based on numbers stated by the US Department of Labor Statistics, the average weekly earnings in 2015 for women who worked full-time jobs (both hourly and salaried) were roughly $726, whereas those of men were around $895. And in 2014, women brought in about 79 percent of what men made.

The wage gaps gape even wider among white-collar jobs, where pay rates depend more on the choice of field, the candidate's ability to negotiate his or her pay, and the manager's subjective impression of the employees and their work. Although discrimination by male managers frequently inhibits the progress of women, plenty of additional elements affect a woman's ability to achieve the same wages as her male counterparts.

PROTECTION WITHIN THE WORKPLACE

The year 1964 saw a landmark decision in the Civil Rights Act of 1964. This act protected women and minorities from discrimination when hiring. In 1977 Canada passed the Human Rights Act made sure that all genders, disabilities, and religions received equal opportunity were not discriminated against. It only applies only to industries that are federally regulated however. Antidiscrimination laws are executed by each individual province.

The Civil Rights Act of 1964 laid the groundwork for a number of major rulings by the US Supreme Court that granted women legal protections in the workplace that they never had before, beginning in the 1970s.

In 1970, in *Schultz v. Wheaton Glass Co.*, the court ruled that jobs do not have to be identical to qualify for equal pay; they merely have to be "substantially equivalent." This was a landmark case because it stopped employers from giving women different job titles and claiming that their jobs were different from jobs being done by men that were essentially the same.

In 1971, in *Phillips v. Martin Marietta Corp.*, the court ruled that a company could not refuse to hire women because they had preschool-aged children, unless it also refused to hire men who had them as well. This was a direct challenge to the concept that women shouldn't be hired because they would neglect their children to work, or neglect their work to take care of their children. That same year, in *Reed v. Reed*, the court struck down an Illinois law that arbitrarily gave preference to men as to who should administer the estate of someone who died without a will. (The case involved the choice of a male parent over a female parent when it came to who should administer the estate of a deceased child.) The court ruled that giving preference to a man over a woman in legal matters, when there was no legitimate reason for doing so, violated the Fourteenth Amendment, which guarantees equal protection under the law to all US citizens.

In 1973, in *Pittsburgh Press Co. v. Pittsburgh Commission on Human Relations*, the court upheld a municipal ordinance that forbade companies from specifying the gender of applicants in want ads for jobs. This was one of the most fundamental changes in hiring practices.

In 1974, in *Corning Glassworks v. Brennan*, the court ruled that women could not be paid a lower wage than men simply because it was what they were customarily paid in the marketplace. This makes sense because this is exactly what the law was trying to address.

Advertisements for jobs are not permitted to call for a specific gender, thanks to the *Pittsburgh Press Co. v. Pittsburgh Commission on Human Relations* case.

Both Congress and the Supreme Court were active in taking steps to reduce discrimination against women. The following are some of the major laws enacted to protect individuals' rights in the workplace—laws that directly affected women.

EQUAL EMPLOYMENT OPPORTUNITY COMMISSION

As the civil rights struggle heightened in the 1960s, President John F. Kennedy announced plans to enact the Civil Rights Act. This was an omnibus bill (which means it contained many provisions) to address discrimination in voting, education, and employment, among other areas. Despite Kennedy's assassination in 1963, Congress passed the act and the Civil Rights Act of 1964 became law. Title VII of the act, which prohibited discrimination based on race, color, national origin, sex, and religion, created the Equal Employment Opportunity Commission (EEOC). The EEOC is charged with enforcing antidiscrimination laws relating to employment and resolving complaints of discrimination.

If you feel that you have been discriminated against, you can file a claim with the Equal Employment Opportunity Commission (EEOC). Claims can be filed in person at an EEOC office or by phone. In areas where state or local agencies exist, you may be required to file a claim with them first. If this is the case, the filing deadline for the EEOC is extended while awaiting results from local agencies. A list of local EEOC offices is available on the internet at https://www.eeoc.gov/field/index.cfm.

EXECUTIVE ORDER 11246

Also contributing to the hiring of an increasing number of women in business is Executive Order 11246, which is administered by the US Labor Department's Office of Federal Contract Compliance

Programs. This order requires firms that do business with the federal government to implement affirmative action and nondiscrimination measures if they want to obtain government contracts. Preference in awarding contracts is given to firms that take steps to hire more minorities and women. This legislation has contributed to an increase in women in traditionally male industries, such as defense, energy, and construction, among others.

THE PREGNANCY DISCRIMINATION ACT

The Pregnancy Discrimination Act, which is an amendment to the 1964 Civil Rights Act, prohibits discrimination against pregnant women. It makes it illegal to refuse to hire a woman because she is pregnant or to keep her from doing her normal job duties because she is pregnant. According to the EEOC, in fiscal year 2011, EEOC received 5,797 charges of pregnancy-based discrimination. Of those, the EEOC was able to resolve 6,482 charges in and recover $17.2 million in monetary benefits.

Another law that has been a help to women is the Family Leave and Medical Act. This law, passed in 1995, provides employees with up to twelve weeks of leave per year for medical purposes, for themselves

The Pregnancy Discrimination Act makes it illegal to refuse to hire a qualified woman or prevent her from doing her duties strictly because she is pregnant.

or to take care of a family member. During this time, the company is required to maintain their health care benefits. Upon completion of their leave, employees are entitled to have their job back or receive an equivalent one. The law applies to state, local, and federal government agencies and companies with more than fifty employees. The provisions include maternity leave and leave to care for a newborn. Although it applies

Lilly Ledbetter stands with President Barack Obama. The Lilly Ledbetter Fair Pay Act allows women to file lawsuits if they find they have been paid less than their male counterparts.

to male employees as well, it is particularly important for women because they are more likely to stay home with a newborn and be the one to care for a sick family member.

LILLY LEDBETTER FAIR PAY ACT

The Lilly Ledbetter Fair Pay Act was passed by Congress, and was the first bill signed into law by President Barack Obama, on January 30, 2009. This bill removes the 180-day limitation on filing suits for discrimination when a woman is paid less than her male colleagues performing the same work. This means that if a woman found out that she had been receiving less pay for the same work for a period of years, she would be able to obtain compensation for past discrimination.

A second bill that was passed by the US House of Representatives in January 2009 is the Paycheck Fairness Act. This act would require an employer to pay women at the same rate as men for a given job unless the employer could demonstrate that there was a reason other than gender (such as education level, skills, or experience) that would justify a pay difference. Further, it would give women the right to sue for punitive damages, not just back pay. Punitive damages are those awarded to a plaintiff (the person who is suing) by a court as punishment of the defendant for breaking a law.

The Paycheck Fairness Act has had a long wait. Two early versions failed in the US Senate (in 2012 and 2014). On March 25, 2015, the bill was reintroduced and where it was awaiting consideration. If it passes in the House or the Senate, it will be sent on to be signed by the president and become law.

STUBBORN INEQUALITIES: THE GLOBAL GAP

The 2015 Global Gender Gap Report, which has been published since 2006, "shows that while the world has made progress overall, stubborn inequalities remain." In 2006, about 1.5 billion women were in the workforce, and that number has crept up to about 1.75 billion in 2015. (Meanwhile, in the same time frame, men increased from 2.25 billion to just over 2.62 billion.) Globally, annual earnings have also increased over the years, from $6,000 (compared to $11,000 by men) in 2006 and now $11,000 by women (and $21,000 by men. "And yet, the annual pay for women only now equals the amount men were earning TEN YEARS AGO."

Out of 145 countries ranked by the report, the United States ranked 28 on the Gender Gap Index 2015. Meanwhile, the United Kingdom came in at 18, followed by South Africa at 17, Canada at 30, and China at 91. Iceland claimed the top spot as number 1. Here are the top and bottom ten countries in the report, according to the British Broadcasting Corporation's (BBC's) Naomi Grimley:

	Top Ten	Bottom Ten
1	Iceland	Yemen
2	Norway	Pakistan
3	Finland	Syria
4	Sweden	Chad
5	Ireland	Iran
6	Rwanda	Jordan
7	Philippines	Morocco
8	Switzerland	Lebanon
9	Slovenia	Mali
10	New Zealand	Egypt

It may be some time before the gaping gap in wages is finally closed up. According to a report by the BBC, the World Economic Forum predicts that by the year 2133 the gap will finally be closed.

CHOOSING YOUR WORK

Some aspects of employment that affect pay are within a woman's control. One reason for the disparity between how much men and women make is the type of fields in which women work. The following is a 2014 list from the US Department of Labor of the top-ten professions in which women are employed. Many of the jobs women choose, such as teaching, place a high premium on emotional fulfillment and a sense of contribution at the expense of less-fulfilling, higher-paying jobs that might be found in business and industry. The top-ten professions include the following:

Occupation	Number of Full-Time Women Employed
Secretaries and administrative assistants	2,215,000
Elementary and middle school teachers	2,196,000
Registered nurses	2,064,000
Nursing, psychiatric, and home health aides	1,200,000
First-line supervisors/managers of retail sales workers	1,022,000
Managers, all other	983,000
Cashiers	921,000
Accountants and auditors	910,000
Receptionists and information clerks	825,000
First-line supervisors of office and administrative support workers	775,000

Since the 1990s, more than half (57 percent) of all bachelor's degrees have been earned by women, as have about half of all science and engineering (S&E) bachelor's degrees, Participation by women in S&E

Elementary and middle school teachers are among the top ten professions for women according to the US Department of Labor's 2014 list.

fields fluctuates, but tends to be more stable over every degree level. Most fields show an increasing number of degrees being awarded to women since 1993. The fewest women seem to major in engineering, computer sciences, and physics. They graduate with about 33 percent of the doctorates in economics and just a bit more than 25 percent of mathematics and statistics doctorates. Because science and engineering jobs typically have high pay ranges, the lack of women in such fields has a significant impact on the average pay of women overall.

MALE MANAGERS

When it comes to getting hired, obtaining equal pay, or being promoted, women faced with a male manager are often at a disadvantage. People tend to feel most comfortable with people like themselves and give preference to such people. Even among men, a manager is most likely to reward those he sees as most like himself. In addition, many men still have preconceptions about women, as discussed earlier, and this affects the way they view their employees. Unfortunately, many men feel threatened by a strong or successful woman, and they react in a negative fashion.

YOU'RE WORTH IT

The fact that the law says it is unfair to discriminate in matters of pay does not mean you can be assured that you are getting the same salary as your coworkers.

Male managers are more likely to hire, promote, and offer equal pay to those most like themselves. Obviously, this puts women at a disadvantage.

For jobs in which workers are paid an hourly wage, it is generally easy to establish what the pay rate is for people with similar years of experience and levels of performance. When it comes to salaried workers, however, it is much more difficult to know how one's pay compares to colleagues'. Often, there is a large range for a given job, such as marketing manager, and in many businesses, how well you negotiate for a starting salary and for raises is the major factor influencing your pay.

TAKING ACTION

One step you can take to protect yourself against discrimination on the job is document the job you're doing. Keep copies of any positive job reviews or evaluations, commendations, or letters from managers, clients, or customers praising your work. Also, document any special achievements or contributions that you make to the company. For example, if you were the top salesperson for the year or came up with a procedure that saved the company a large sum of money, document this.

A company is under no obligation to spend more money than it has to. In fact, managers are often rewarded for keeping costs down. The fact is that one of the major reasons men make more money than women in the same position is that they ask for it. Women are often more reluctant to confront managers about their pay because they don't like conflict, are afraid they may not be worth more, or have an unrealistic fear that they will lose their job if they ask for more. Let's address these issues.

First, if you ask for a raise, promotion, special assignment that's available, or anything else in a

When asking for a special assignment at work, acting professional and calm will help keep the conversation positive and better your chances for the outcome you'd like.

nonconfrontational and professional manner, it's unlikely that the discussion will turn unpleasant. You might get what you want or not, but if you can't have what you want, your manager will most likely explain why it's not possible. And you can accept that or take the next appropriate step.

It's also highly unlikely that you'll be fired just for asking for more compensation if you take a professional approach. It takes a lot of time and money to train someone new for a position in an organization. If you are doing a good job, you are a useful asset to the company. For that reason, if your manager doesn't want to pay you more, he or she will most likely either explain why that's not possible or promise to review your situation at a later date. If the latter is the case, have your manger pencil in a precise date on the calendar so that you are not fobbed off with the same excuse every time you ask.

The issue of what one is worth is decidedly more difficult. In reality, what many women don't realize is that this question is entirely irrelevant. If you are doing a good job and haven't received a raise in some time, or if you find that other people in your position are making more, simply do what many men do: go to your boss, point this fact out (in a professional tone), show him your evidence of contribution, and ask for more.

Keeping track of the job you're doing has another use as well. If you feel that you deserved a promotion over a coworker or did not get as high a raise as male coworkers who do similar work, this documentation will back up your argument that you have been treated unfairly. And you will feel good for standing up for what you deserve. You're worth it.

UNPROTECTED

Unfortunately, many women are almost completely unprotected at work around the world. In fact, according to an article for Human Rights Watch by Nisha Varia, "Only 10% of domestic workers worldwide are employed in countries that extend them equal protection under national labour laws. Some 30% work in countries ranging from the United Arab Emirates to Singapore that exclude domestic workers from labour laws completely, leaving them without such basic protections as a minimum wage, overtime pay, rest days, or social security. Others, such as the United States, fall somewhere in between, for example by guaranteeing a minimum wage but denying domestic workers the right to form unions."

Po Pov works in a Cambodian garment factory. She explains, "It doesn't matter whether you are pregnant or not—whether you are sick or not—you have to sit and work. If you take a break, the work piles up on the machine and the supervisor will come and shout. And if a pregnant worker is seen as working 'slowly,' her contract won't be renewed." Even in the last ten years workers around the world have been forced to endure these conditions and more, such as excessively long working hours. They may be confined to the place where they work. They may not even be paid for all the work they do. Young girls are sometimes forced into labor. Efforts to form labor unions that might help them negotiate for fair and equal treatment are quashed. And sexual abuse and harassment is all too common as well.

CHAPTER 5

HANDLING WORKPLACE SEXUAL HARASSMENT

A discussion about sexual harassment in the workplace should first begin with a clear definition of what constitutes sexual harassment. According to the US Equal Employment Opportunity Commission (EEOC), "Harassment can include 'sexual harassment' or unwelcome sexual advances, requests for sexual favors, and other verbal or physical harassment of a sexual nature." Any conduct that suggests that an employee's continued employment is contingent on providing sexual favors is sexual harassment. Offensive comments and jokes as well as physical behavior can fall into the category as well.

Unwanted verbal or physical sexual advances or harassment, requests for sexual favors, or offensive comments and jokes all fall within the definition of sexual harassment.

According to the courts, if management does not act to put an end to sexual harassment, then they are responsible for creating a hostile work environment for the women who have to put up with it.

HANDLING HARASSMENT

If you feel that someone is sexually harassing you or is behaving inappropriately, there are certain steps you must take to both physically and legally protect yourself.

IDENTIFYING SEXUAL HARASSMENT

Here are a number of key points about sexual harassment:

- Sexual harassment is not dependent on gender. The harasser and victim can be of either gender.
- The harasser does not have to be a supervisor, or even an employee of the company. A manager,

(continued on the next page)

(continued from the previous page)

coworker, or non-employee like an outside contractor can engage in sexual harassment. It is up to the company to protect the employee from sexual harassment, regardless of the source.

- In addition to the person who is directly harassed, other people affected by the conduct may be considered victims of sexual harassment.

- Sexual harassment does not have to involve loss of money or job. Hostile or offensive behavior is still harassment, even if there is no financial cost to the victim.

- The behavior must be unwanted to be sexual harassment. If two people are interested in each other and decide to date, this is not illegal. However, because such lines are not always clear, one should be very careful about approaching someone else in the workplace, and consider what might happen if the relationship doesn't work out. It is rarely advisable for a supervisor to approach a subordinate with a romantic interest.

BE CLEAR

First, it is important to make it clear to the harasser that the behavior is unwelcome. Many people have a juvenile or inappropriate sense of humor, and their buddies often share this. If people say things that are offensive to you, or they make off-color jokes, tell them that you find those things offensive. If someone approaches you inappropriately, make it clear that

Always make it clear that the attention is unwanted if someone's actions are inappropriate, especially if you feel he or she is sexually harassing you.

you are not interested and/or object to that person's behavior. This is important in establishing that the behavior is unwelcome.

DOCUMENT EVERYTHING

Once the incident is over, immediately write down what happened, when it happened, where it happened, who was present, and exactly what was said or done. That way, you will have all the facts and won't have to worry about forgetting the exact details of the incident.

TALK TO YOUR EMPLOYER

Before you do anything else, discuss the situation with your employer. Companies have a vested interest in complying with the law. There are laws against sexual harassment, and the company has nothing to gain—and a lot to lose—by violating them. Do not assume that your boss or other members of management are aware that there is a problem. Start by informing them about the situation. Do so in a straightforward manner, without being confrontational. Take the approach that there is a problem and you want to work with management to resolve it.

Next, you should access whatever mechanism your company has to deal with sexual harassment. Your company should have a process for dealing with complaints about sexual harassment. The human

Reach out to your employer, perhaps by way of the human resources department, if you are the victim of sexual harassment. They should be able to help file a complaint.

resources department should be able to tell you exactly what you should do to file a complaint.

SEEK OUTSIDE HELP

If the situation is not resolved appropriately, contact the EEOC for information on how to file a sexual harassment complaint, or consult a lawyer who deals with sexual harassment issues. Every company is required to have procedures in place to deal with sexual harassment and to take immediate steps to deal with it when it occurs. Failure to do so is cause for filing a sexual harassment suit. This should be your last step. If you need to file a suit, you will need to hire a lawyer.

Standing up for your rights when you have experienced sexual harassment may be extremely difficult, and many women are afraid or embarrassed to report such incidents. No one deserves to work in a place where they are harassed or abused in any way.

10 GREAT QUESTIONS TO ASK A HUMAN RESOURCES REPRESENTATIVE

1. What is the company's policy on sexual harassment?
2. Is what occurred in this particular incident considered sexual harassment?
3. How should I proceed?
4. What kind of documentation do I need to prove sexual harassment?
5. What should I do if the person who did it, or his or her friends, retaliates against me?
6. Do you have a list of counselors that I can speak to about my experience?
7. What kind of response should I reasonably expect from the company?
8. When can I expect a response?
9. What steps will the company take to discipline the person who did it?
10. What should I do if the person repeats his actions?

CHAPTER 6

ISSUES IN THE ARMED FORCES

In the military, women face a whole new set of circumstances and issues unlike any they faced as civilians. Women in the armed forces are affected by a number of rulings and specific issues.

WOMEN'S SERVICES INTEGRATION ACT

On June 12, 1948, Congress passed the Women's Services Integration Act. This act allows women to serve as regular members of the US Army, Navy, Marine Corps, and Air Force on the same footing as men. In 1951,

Secretary of Defense George C. Marshall formed the Defense Department Advisory Committee on Women in the Services to help protect and support military women.

Secretary of Defense George C. Marshall formed the Defense Department Advisory Committee on Women in the Services. This committee is still active, and it advises the Defense Department on regulations needed to ensure the proper recruiting, training, retaining, and employing of women, and ensuring the proper treatment of women in the military. The committee's recommendations have served as the basis for changes in many of the regulations and procedures in the military. The following are some of the committee's recommendations:

- In 1978, they recommended that the Navy and Marine Corps allow women to be commissioned as limited duty officers. A limited duty officer is someone who is promoted from the ranks because he or she possesses a certain technical skill that is needed. These officers are limited in the rank that they can advance to, hence the title limited duty officer. Prior to 1978, the Limited Duty Officer Program was only open to men.
- In 1979, they made two recommendations that affect women in the military today. These include the recommendation that the eligibility standards for women be the same as for men, except for obvious physical differences. In addition, there should be identical standards for promotion of men and women in the Marine Corps.

- In 1980, they recommended that the president of the United States give priority to the appointment of women as judges to the US Court of Military Appeals. Currently, the court includes female judges, including one senior judge.
- In 1984, they recommended that the secretary of defense publish a formal policy requiring commanders to fully use women in their units.
- In 1992, they recommended that the secretary of defense allow women pilots in all military services on equal footing with men. The Navy had

Lieutenant Judith Ann Neuffer was one of the first six female pilots to be sworn into the US Navy in 1974.

broken the sex barrier by swearing in six women pilots as naval aviators in 1974, and the Air Force had followed suit in 1976. But women were only allowed to fly in noncombat situations. Beginning in 1993, women were allowed to fly in combat.

- In 1993, they recommended that women be integrated into all military ceremonial units such as ceremonial guard units and the Army Drill Team. They also recommended that Pathfinder training be open to women as well as men. Pathfinders guide paratroopers (airborne soldiers) to parachute drop zones.
- In 1996, they recommended that the Navy open to women all types of ships and vessels.
- In 1999, they recommended that women be allowed into the Special Operations Forces (those involved in scouting, special operations, and counterterrorism). Today, women are serving in the US Special Forces Command.
- In 2016 they recommended that the Secretary of Defense require the Office of General Counsel to review the Marine Corps Performance Evaluation System (PES), including "annotating pregnancy on the PES form."
- In 2016, sexual harassment and sexual assault training was listed as a continuing concern, as was the accessibility of maternity uniforms for pregnant solders.

ARMED FORCES DISCRIMINATION

By choosing to enter what has traditionally been a male-dominated field, women are likely to encounter many men who perceive them as weaker and who question how they will hold up under the stress of military life. This is a particular concern for women who are sent into combat areas. Even though the US military does not place women in direct combat, their support positions often bring them into danger, especially when serving in areas like Iraq and Afghanistan, where enemy combatants may be anywhere.

Many men in the military come from traditional households where the men do physical labor and the women take care of the home and children. Such men may have difficultly accepting a woman as capable of being a soldier in the same way that a man is. In the military, people's lives may depend on the behavior and responses of their colleagues. Men may see a woman as likely to break under the emotional stress of combat and thus put his life in danger. Others may see women as causing men to act less tough and aggressive—behaviors they see as part of the warrior creed, as well as critical to maintaining their fighting edge.

Such attitudes led to some major incidents when women first began entering the military in significant numbers. Women have historically faced the most resistance to their presence in the Marine Corps, a service whose male participants have long viewed themselves as elite warriors. In 1991, the Women's Services Integration Act recommended that the Marine Corps address policies that keep women from being fully accepted in the Marines. Recommendations included the removal of gender-specific labels such as "women marines," elimination of differences in training, and an increase in the number of female instructors used to train male recruits. They also suggested eliminating the slogan "A Few Good Men" from Marine recruitment campaigns.

MILITARY COLLEGE CONCERNS

Women have faced serious discrimination in major military colleges and academies, both in getting admitted and in the treatment that they receive after they arrive. The Military College of South Carolina, better known as the Citadel, is one of six military colleges around the United States. It provides military-style training as well as academic courses, and roughly 30 percent of its graduates enter the armed forces. It became notorious in 1995 when a female applicant, Shannon Faulkner, who was denied admission, engaged in a lawsuit against the institution. Faulkner won her suit and entered the college. A week later, she quit. She cited psychological abuse, among other reasons. The Citadel dropped its all-male policy shortly thereafter, however, because the Supreme Court ruled against the Virginia Military Institute, which likewise had an all-male policy. Four women were admitted, but trouble continued. In 1996, the Citadel suspended a cadet and relieved five others of their commands because of the harassment of female cadets. In 1999, Nancy Mace became the first woman to graduate from the Citadel. Yet a 2006 study revealed that harassment continues to be a problem for women, with nearly 20 percent of the

Discrimination against women in military education institutions has run rampant, but in 1999 Nancy Mace became the first woman to graduate from the Citadel.

female cadets reporting that they have been assaulted. Half of the women said that they didn't report incidents for fear of being further harassed. Sixty-eight percent of the women reported one or more incidents of sexual harassment, including sexual stories, jokes, and offensive remarks.

Similar problems have occurred at academies charged with training officers for US military services. Despite the fact that the Air Force Academy has been admitting women since 1976, it has had repeated problems. In 2003, a sexual assault scandal erupted at the Air Force Academy in Colorado Springs, Colorado, which led to the firing of the academy's leadership. Nearly 150 women claimed to have been abused there between 1993 and 2003. Despite the fact that the situation led to a review of the military's policy on sexual assault, a 2005 survey of cadets revealed that 22 percent of male cadets did not believe that women belonged at the academy.

The US Military Academy at West Point, which trains US Army officers, has experienced similar problems with sexual harassment. About 15 percent of the academy's four thousand cadets are women. A survey revealed that about 10 percent of the female cadets reported incidents of sexual harassment. West Point began admitting women in 1976. In 1990, Kristin Baker became the first female First Captain, the cadet brigade commander at West Point. The appointment

When Kristin Baker became West Point's first female First Captain, she was in charge of all cadets. Some males objected to taking orders from a woman.

is given to the student deemed to excel in athletic, academic, and leadership ability. The First Captain is essentially the boss of all cadets. Not everyone thought this was a positive step. Not only were some male cadets resistant to taking orders from a woman, but the academy also received a slew of letters from West Point alumni objecting to the appointment of a woman as First Captain.

In response to the problems experienced by female cadets, the House Armed Services Committee of the US Congress created a task force in 2004 to investigate the issue at the Air Force, Military, and Naval academies. All the academies have instituted zero-tolerance policies for sexual abuse, and West Point now provides special advocates and counselors for women who experience sexual abuse.

In 2012, male cadets separately reported complaints against a male former cadet regarding four incidents of assault and attacks, for example. This can be an important reminder that both women and men experience assault and harassment in the workplace and in the military. While it's a far more frequent issue for women and other minorities, anyone can experience this kind of negative treatment, no matter what their gender, race, or sexual preference. And it's never OK.

CHAPTER 7

LOOKING FORWARD

Women have made tremendous strides in the fight toward a simple achievement: equal treatment at work. Nevertheless, a maddeningly wide chasm still yawns between the ways men and women are treated in the workplace. In some cases, cultural convictions need to be adjusted; in others, women need to stand up and take a strong stance when their rights are at risk. Still others, do necessitate further legislation and stronger federal agencies to impose them.

THE OUTLOOK FOR WOMEN AND WORK

The US Department of Labor predicts that by 2050, almost 48 percent of the workforce will be female. If women

Women can make significant workplace progress if they become more of a presence in fields previously dominated by men, such as veterinary medicine.

want to make real progress in the workplace, they will need to expand their presence into other fast-growing scientific and high-technology fields that tend to be dominated by men, such as engineering and information technology (computer hardware, software, and services), veterinary medicine, personal financial advice, forensic science technology, and environmental science.

THE BLACK AND WHITE IN WORKPLACE OBSTACLES

Women are not a single group, all of whom are the same. Women's prospects for achieving equality with men in the workplace can be influenced by factors other than gender. Princeton Research Associates conducted a survey for YWCA USA on the concerns of women from ages eighteen to seventy. They found a significant difference between the concerns of white women and those of black women in regard to workplace issues. When researchers asked subjects if they feared that certain factors would be obstacles to their progress in the workplace over the coming decade, they received the following responses from African American and white women, respectively:

- Major illness or medical expense (84 percent vs. 68 percent)
- Unequal pay (81 percent vs. 55 percent)
- Affordable and accessible childcare (72 percent vs. 57 percent)
- Limited opportunities for job promotion and advancement (72 percent vs. 41 percent)
- Lack of job-training opportunities (66 percent vs. 37 percent)

(continued on the next page)

(continued from the previouspage)

- Student loan indebtedness (62 percent vs. 33 percent)

These results support the idea that white women have a more optimistic view of their present and future position in the workplace than black women do, especially given that almost 60 percent of white women did not think that their opportunity for promotion or advancement would be limited, whereas 72 percent of black women did.

One issue affecting the growth of the number of women in the workforce is the state of the economy. After the housing and stock market crashes of 2008, the economy took a serious downturn. As sales fell, businesses started laying off employees, and unemployment began to rise. Women are particularly vulnerable in economic downturns. First, they are more likely to be employed in part-time positions, which are often the first jobs cut. Second, in positions where seniority is an issue, the fact that women have been hired in large numbers only recently means they are likely to have less seniority and thus be laid off before men who have been in their positions longer. In addition, companies are more willing to invest in non-core business activities, such as human resources initiatives, when the economy is good and they are making a lot of money. During economic downturns, companies focus on reducing costs. As a result, they often cut back on staff and programs in areas like human resources. Or they employ staff on issues such as coping with layoffs, rather than on improving the lot of workers.

BUSINESS OWNERS

Many women in recent years have started their own businesses. There are many reasons for this, but one is the feeling that they have reached the limit to which their present employer will promote them. The nature of women-owned businesses reveals much about the nature of women in the workplace in general.

Women starting their own businesses is the fastest-growing economic trend in the United States. This in itself reflects both women's desire to expand their opportunities beyond what is offered in their present job and the frustration that many feel at the limited opportunities available. According to the National Association of Business Owners, as of 2015, women owned more than 9.4 million business firms. Those companies provide jobs for almost 8 million people and by 2015 had brought in a whopping $1.5 trillion in sales. Women of color own 2.9 million US firms, which employ 1.4 million workers. Twenty percent of all forms making $1 million or more is owned by a woman, and more than 4 percent of all companies owned by women make more than $1 million. Clearly, those are some positive numbers; numbers that might general hope for the future.

One aspect of women-owned businesses may surprise you. Although one might think that college-educated women primarily start these businesses, one-third of women who start their own businesses have high school degrees but not college degrees. Another clear trend is that the percentage of businesses owned by minority women is rising faster than any other segment. The Bureau of Labor Statistics reports that "among women ages 25 to 64 who are in the labor force, the proportion with a college degree more than tripled from 1970 to 2012. Women's earnings as a

Women-owned businesses are becoming more popular. When their employers are reluctant to promote them, owning a business offers more opportunities.

proportion of men's earnings also have grown over time. In 1979, women working full time earned 62 percent of what men earned; in 2012, women's earnings were 81 percent of men's."

One thing is clear, though, as Americans move through the twenty-first century: it is likely that the trend to open businesses will continue, and at least some $1 million-plus women-owned businesses started in recent years will continue to grow and become more influential in the marketplace.

IMPROVEMENTS WITH TECHNOLOGY

One aspect of modern life that is improving women's earning power in the marketplace is technology. The discrepancy between men's and women's pay is greatest at the extremes of the work spectrum—in unskilled and semiskilled jobs, and in senior management, where women have had great difficulties breaking through the glass ceiling. In professional, technical, and middle-management positions, however, women have made significant strides. In such positions, technological skill rather than brute strength is often the determiner of success, and pay scales in such areas are likely to be closer for men and women. In addition, obtaining the highest pay in such areas depends more on factors under

Women still struggle to break through the glass ceiling and achieve senior management positions, a road that may require longer hours at the expense of other parts of their lives.

the control of women: choice of work environment and skill in negotiating. For example, a doctor in a private group practice is likely to make more money than one working for a health maintenance organization (HMO). But she will have to assume more risk if the business fails, and she'll probably have to work longer hours. Thus, there is a trade-off between earning the maximum amount of money and having security, and it is up to the individual woman to decide where she is most comfortable. There is often a tacit assumption that women should want to maximize their income at the expense of other aspects of their lives, but this is not necessarily the best decision for everyone—male or female.

In 1999, the percentage of adult women in the workplace peaked at about 60 percent, according to the Bureau of Labor Statistics. It has been in a decline ever since, although the numbers are still high compared to those in the past. Numbers will ebb and flow over the years, but the important matter is that women continue to work for and gain equality in the workforce.

GLOSSARY

CEO Chief executive officer; the highest-ranking manager in a company.

CIVIL RIGHTS ACT OF 1964 Legislation that made it illegal to discriminate on the basis of race or gender.

DEPRESSION A downturn in the economy.

DEXTERITY Fine hand control.

EEOC Equal Employment Opportunity Commission, the federal organization that deals with issues related to workplace discrimination.

FORTUNE 500 A list of the five hundred largest companies in the United States, compiled annually by the business magazine *Fortune*.

INFORMATION TECHNOLOGY The field of computer hardware, software, and services.

LABOR UNION An organized group of workers who work together to protect their rights in the workplace.

MIDDLE MANAGEMENT Managers responsible for directly supervising employees or managing specific day-to-day functions of a company.

OMNIBUS BILL A bill that is made up of a number of items.

PLAINTIFF A person who brings a lawsuit against a company or another person.

PRECONCEPTION An assumption formed before examining the facts.

PREDOMINANT Major or primary.

PREINDUSTRIAL Describing the time when most goods were made by hand, rather than by machine.

PROHIBIT To forbid.

PROSPEROUS Being comfortable and well-off.

RETAIL TRADE The area of business in which items are sold to people.

S&P 500 Short for the Standard & Poor's Index's group of 500 companies. The S&P bases their index on the prices of the shares of these companies.

SENIOR MANAGEMENT The highest level of management in a business, usually vice presidents and chief executive, operating, and financial officers.

SUPREME COURT The highest court in the United States; it decides whether or not rulings by lower courts comply with the US Constitution.

SWEATSHOP A factory or workshop where employees are forced to work in terrible conditions.

WOMEN'S MOVEMENT The organized effort by women to change the way they are perceived and treated.

TACIT Understood without being stated.

TEXTILE MILL A factory that makes cloth from thread or yarn.

Equal Rights Advocates
1170 Market Street, Suite 700
San Francisco, CA 94102
(415) 621-0672
Website: http://www.equalrights.org/
Equal Rights Advocates focuses on equal rights and economic opportunity for women and girls. It provides counseling and legal assistance, as well as publications.

National Organization of Women (NOW)
1100 H Street, #300
Washington, DC 20005
(202) 628-8669 (628-8NOW)
Website: http://www.now.org
NOW is the premiere organization working to promote women's rights. Its Web site provides a list of local chapters and news on women's issues.

9to5
207 East Buffalo Street, Suite #211
Milwaukee WI 53202
(414) 274-0925
Website: http://www.9to5.org
This organization is focused on bettering the lot and winning equal treatment for working women, especially those working in traditional female occupations.

Women's Bureau
US Department of Labor
200 Constitution Avenue NW, Room S-3002 Washington, DC 20210
(800) 827-5335
Website: http://www.dol.gov/wb
The Department of Labor provides information for women and reports on a wide range of topics relating to women in the workplace.

US Equal Employment Opportunity Commission
131 M Street NE
Washington, DC 20507
(202) 663-4900
Website: http://www.eeoc.gov
The EEOC assists women filing claims for discrimination. Its website provides detailed information on women's rights in the workplace.

Women Work!
1625 K Street NW, Suite 300
Washington, DC 20006
(800) 235-2732; (202) 467-6346
Website: http://www.womenwork.org
This is a nonprofit organization that seeks to help women obtain jobs and improve their position in the workplace. It provides a variety of printed and online resources.

Workplace Fairness
8121 Georgia Avenue, Suite 600
Silver Spring, MD 20910
(240) 772-1205
Website: http://www.workplacefairness.org
Workplace Fairness is an organization that provides resources for working people. It releases an electronic newsletter, information on court decisions, and information on attorneys.

WEBSITES

Because of the changing nature of internet links, Rosen Publishing has developed an online list of websites related to the subject of this book. This site is updated regularly. Please use this link to access this list:

http://www.rosenlinks.com/WITW/work

FOR FURTHER READING

Bolles, Richard Nelson, Carol Christen, and Jean M. Blomquist. *What Color Is Your Parachute for Teens—Discovering Yourself, Defining Your Future*, 3rd ed. Berkeley, CA: Ten Speed Press, 2016.

Day, Meredith. *A Primary Source Investigation of Women's Suffrage* (Uncovering American History). New York, NY: Rosen Central, 2016.

Ehrenreich, Barbara. *Nickel and Dimed: On (Not) Getting by in America.* New York, NY: Picador, 2011.

Gillard, Arthur. *Sexual Harassment*. New York, NY: Greenhaven Publishing, 2014.

Hawker, Louise. *Women's Rights*. New York, NY: Greenhaven Publishing, 2010.

Justice Learning. *The United States Constitution: What it Says, What it Means*. New York, NY: Oxford University Press, 2005.

Kamberg, Mary-Lane. *Affirmative Action.* New York, NY: Rosen Young Adult, 2015.

Niver, Heather Moore. *Women and Networking Leveraging the Sisterhood* (A Young Woman's Guide to Contemporary Issues). New York, NY: Rosen Young Adult, 2013.

Lowery, Zoe, and Jenny MacBain. *A Primary Source Investigation of the Salem Witch Trials* (Uncovering American History). New York, NY: Rosen Central, 2016.

Seligson, Hannah. *New Girl on the Job: Advice from the Trenches*. New York, NY: Kensington, 2014.

Slomka, Beverly F. *Teens and the Job Game: Prepare Today—Win It Tomorrow*. Bloomington, IN: iUniverse, 2011.

Turk, Katherine. *Equality on Trial: Gender and Rights in the Modern American Workplace*. Philadelphia, PA: University of Pennsylvania Press, 2016.

BIBLIOGRAPHY

"25 Most Common Occupations for Employed Women by Selected Characteristics (2014 Annual Averages)." US Department of Labor, Retrieved December 1, 2016. https://www.dol.gov/wb/stats/25mostcommon_occs_employ_women_txt.htm.

"2016 Recommendations & Continuing Concerns." Defense Department Advisory Committee on Women in the Services. http://dacowits.defense.gov/Portals/48/Documents/General%20Documents/DACOWITS%202016%20Recommendations%20and%20Continuing%20Concerns.pdf?ver=2016-09-14-151419-627.

Associated Press. "Working Women Do More Chores Than Men." September 14, 2004. http://www.msnbc.msn.com/id/6011245.

Baxandall, Rosalyn, Lynda Gordon, and Susan Reverby. *America's Working Women: A Documentary History 1600 to the Present*. New York, NY: Random House, 1976.

Bonné, Jon. "A Gender Split in the Executive Suite." MSNBC, August 11, 2004. http://www.msnbc.msn.com/id/5624773.

Bureau of Labor Statistics . "Current Population Survey (CPS)/ Graph by the Women's Bureau, U.S. Department of Labor. "Civilian Labor Force by Sex, 1970–2012." Retrieved November 29, 2016. https://www.dol.gov/wb/stats/

Civilian_labor_force_sex_70_12_txt.htm.

"Breaking Down the Gender Wage Gap." Bureau of Labor Statistics, April 2016. GenderWageGap-2pager_6_9_16.pdf.

Canada Department of Human Resource Development. "Gender Composition and Wages: Why Is Canada Different from the United States?" March 2000. http://www.hrsdc.gc.ca/eng/cs/sp/hrsd/prc/publications/research/2000-000181/page00.shtml.

Catalyst. *Women CEOs of the S&P 500*. New York, NY: Catalyst, September 30, http://www.catalyst.org/knowledge/women-ceos-sp-500.

Catalyst. *Pyramid: Women in S&P 500 Companies*. New York, NY: Catalyst, September 19, 2016. http://www.catalyst.org/knowledge/women-sp-500-companies.

"Citadel Dealing with More Charges of Sex Abuse." WCIV ABC News 4. September 18, 2012. http://abcnews4.com/archive/citadel-dealing-with-more-charges-of-sex-abuse,.

"Charts by Topic: Household Activities." Bureau of Labor Statistics, October 26, http://www.bls.gov/TUS/CHARTS/HOUSEHOLD.HTM.

Equal Employment Opportunity Commission. "Filing a Charge." Retrieved January 12, 2009. http://www.eeoc.gov/facts/howtofil.html.

Equal Employment Opportunity Commission.

"Sexual Harassment." Retrieved January 12, 2009. http://www.eeoc.gov/facts/fs-sex.html.

Farrell, Warren. *Why Men Earn More*. New York, NY: American Management Association, 2005.

"Field of Degree: Women." National Science Foundation, January 2015 https://www.nsf.gov/statistics/2015/nsf15311/digest/theme2.cfm#economics.

Gillis, Deborah. "The Politics of Women in Leadership." Catalyst, October 25, 2016. http://www.catalyst.org/blog/catalyzing/politics-women-leadership.

Grant Thornton. "Four in Ten Businesses Worldwide Have No Women in Senior Management." 2007. http://www.grantthorntonibos.com/Press-room/2007/women-in-senior-management.asp.

Grimley, Naomi. "Gender Pay Gap 'May Take 118 Years to Close' - World Economic Forum." BBC News, November 19, 2015. http://www.bbc.com/news/world-europe-34842471.

Human Rights Watch. "Domestic Workers." 2012. https://www.hrw.org/topic/womens-rights/domestic-workers.

International Labor Rights Forum. "Women's Rights." Retrieved November 30, 2016. http://www.laborrights.org/issues/women%E2%80%99s-rights.

Kaufman, Gil. "Many Female Cadets at Citadel

Reporting Sexual Assault." MTV, August 26, 2006. http://www.mtv.com/news/articles/1539311/20060824/story.jhtml.

"Labor Force Statistics from the Current Population Survey." Bureau of Labor Statistics, February 10, 2016. http://www.bls.gov/cps/cpsaat39.htm.

Lyness, Karen S., and Madeline E. Heilman. "When Fit Is Fundamental: Performance Evaluations and Promotions of Upper-Level Female and Male Managers." *Journal of Applied Psychology*, Vol. 91, No. 4, 2006. pp. 777–785. http://www.uwindsor.ca/users/f/fsirois/GradAppl.nsf/9d019077a3c4f6768525698a00593654/6c9e6979bbb25cac85256e1d006734ca/$FILE/Lyness_2006.pdf.

McCullough, D.G. "When Will Women Achieve Gender Equality in Leadership at Work?" Guardian. June 4, 2014. https://www.theguardian.com/sustainable-business/women-leadership-companies-equality-jobs.

Maria, Nisha. "This Is How Women Are Exploited in Today's Global Workforce. Human Rights Watch, March 8, 2016. https://www.hrw.org/news/2016/03/08/how-women-are-exploited-todays-global-workforce.Pear, Robert. "House Passes 2 Measures on Job Bias." *New York Times*, January 10, 2009, p. A13.

Pear, Robert. "House Passes 2 Measures on Job Bias." New York Times, January 10, 2009, p. A13.

"Pregnancy Discrimination Charges." EEOC Retrieved December 1, 2016. https://www.eeoc.gov/eeoc/statistics/enforcement/pregnancy.cfm.

"Pregnancy Discrimination Charges." EEOC Retrieved December 1, 2016. https://www.eeoc.gov/eeoc/statistics/enforcement/pregnancy.cfm.

"President Obama Signs Executive Order Protecting LGBT People from Workplace Discrimination." ACLU, July 21, 2014. https://www.aclu.org/news/president-obama-signs-executive-order-protecting-lgbt-people-workplace-discrimination?redirect=lgbt-rights/president-obama-signs-executive-order-protecting-lgbt-people-workplace-discrimination.

PR Newswire. "YWCA Survey Shows Greater Economic Concerns Among Black Women Than White Women." January 2009. http://findarticles.com/p/articles/mi_m4PRN/is_2009_Jan_13/ai_n31188076.

Repa, Barbara Kate. *Your Rights in the Workplace*. Berkeley, CA: Nolo, 2007.

"S. 862 — 114th Congress: Paycheck Fairness Act." www.GovTrack.us. 2015. December 2, https://www.govtrack.us/congress/bills/114/s862.

Spraggins, Renee. "Current Population Reports: Men and Women in the U.S." March 2002. Washington, DC:

U.S. Department of Commerce, Census Bureau. http://www.census.gov/prod/2003pubs/p20-544.pdf.

Sutherland, Daniel E. *The Expansion of Everyday Life 1860–1876*. New York, NY: Harper, 1990.

U.S. Department of Labor. "10 Top Jobs for Women," 2007. http://www.dol.gov/wb/factsheets/20lead2007.htm.

U.S. Department of Labor Bureau of Labor Statistics. "Highlights of Women's Earnings in 2007." October 2008. http://www.bls.gov/cps/cpswom2007.pdf.

U.S. Department of Labor Women's Bureau. "Employment Status of Women and Men in 2007." January 7, 2009. http://www.dol.gov/wb/factsheets/Qf-ESWM07.htm.

"Women Business Owner Statistics." National Association of Business Owners. 2015. https://www.nawbo.org/resources/women-business-owner-statistics.

"Women in the Labor Force: A Data Book." US Bureau of Labor Statistics, May 2014. www.bls.gov/cps/wlf-databook-2013.pdf.

World Economic Forum. "Economies." 2016. http://reports.weforum.org/global-gender-gap-report-2015/economies/#economy=ZAF.

INDEX

ABOUT THE AUTHORS

Zoe Lowery is an avid student of history, with a particular interest in women's roles. When she's not writing or editing, Lowery enjoys experimenting with recipes in the kitchen or riding her motorcycle over the mountains or to her local library in Colorado.

Jeri Freedman earned a BA degree from Harvard University. For fifteen years, she worked in administrative and managerial positions in high-technology companies. Among her responsibilities were running employee training programs and creating audiovisual training materials. Among the previous books she has written for young adults are *Privacy vs. Security* and *Cyber Citizenship: Intellectual Property*.

PHOTO CREDITS

Cover StockLite/Shutterstock.com; pp. 8-9 Big Cheese Photo/ Thinkstock; p. 11 Florilegius/SSPL/Getty Images; p. 13 Popperfoto/ Getty Images; p. 15 Past Pix/SSPL/Getty Images; p. 20 Historical/ Corbis Historical/Getty Images; p. 23 CBS Photo Archive/CBS/ Getty Images; p. 26 michaeljung/iStock/Thinkstock; p. 30 Barbara Alper/Archive Photos/Getty Images; p. 32 Andrey Bondarets/ Shutterstock.com; p. 36 Photographee.eu/Shutterstock.com; p. 43 iofoto/Shutterstock.com; p. 50 zimmytws/iStock/Thinkstock; p. 53 monkeybusinessimages/iStock/Thinkstock; p. 54 Mark Wilson/Getty Images; p. 59 A and N photography/Shutterstock.com; p. 61 Iakov Filimonov/Shutterstock.com; p. 63 Rawpixel.com/Shutterstock.com; p. 68 nixite/iStock/Thinkstock; p. 71 microgen/iStock/Thinkstock; p. 73 DragonImages/iStock/Thinkstock; p. 77 ullstein bild/ Getty Images; p. 79 Bettmann/Getty Images; p. 83 © AP Images; p. 85 Arty Pomerantz/ New York Post/Photo Archives, LLC/Getty Images; p. 88 fotoedu/ iStock/Thinkstock; p. 92 © iStockphoto.com/PeopleImages; p. 94 bowdenimages/ iStock/Thinkstock; cover and interior pages (globe) LuckyDesigner/Shutterstock.com; cover and interior pages background designs lulias/Shutterstock.com, Dawid Lech/Shutterstock.com, Transia Design/Shutterstock.com.

Designer: Nicole Russo-Duca; Editor: Heather Moore Niver
Photo Researcher: Heather Moore Niver